From: _____

To: _____

Date: _____

In Loving Memory of:

_____

Dear Brave Friend

Written by Leigh Ann Gerk MA, LPC
Illustrated by Trish Murtha

Illustrations: Trish Murtha
Editor: Catherine Cattarello

Managing Editor: Robin Shukle
Design and Production: Liz Mrofka

Printed by Kindle Direct Publishing

Golden Harvest Publishing
Loveland, CO 80538
MourningtoLightPetLoss.com

ISBN-13: 9781089400691

Dedication

I have loved and lost many beloved pets throughout my life, but there was one special, silly boy named Teddy who changed my life forever. Our time together was priceless; from your love of being dressed up to the special way you woke me up in the morning by gently touching my hand. The day you left me was one of the saddest days of my life. Through losing you, I became inspired to help others who are struggling with the loss of their precious pets. Because of you, I've found my passion and I thank you from the bottom of my heart for giving me such a beautiful, departing gift. You live on through my work every single day . . .

Dear Brave Friend,

Do you know what the word brave means?

It means getting through a really hard time, no matter how much it hurts, and knowing you're going to be okay.

Like you feel when you get a shot at the doctor's office or begin your first day of school.

That is what you are doing right now, you are being brave.

I know you miss me, and I miss you too.
I miss you a lot. It sure was hard to see you cry,
and I'm sorry I made your heart hurt. Mine hurt too,
but I'm going to share a little secret with you—
you may not be able to see me, but I'm still here
with you, just in a different way.

A friendship like ours will last forever.

I want you to put your hand over your heart and listen to it **THUMP, THUMP, THUMP**.

That, my
forever friend,
is my tail wagging
because I'm living
in your heart.

There may be times when you think of
me and smile or even laugh out loud.
Like you used to do when I covered your
face with my wet kisses or stole your socks.

It will make me jump for joy to see you laughing because even though you miss me, you are remembering the fun times we had together. Those memories are your very own and they will continue to grow and be safely tucked away in your heart.

There may be times when you think of me and it makes you sad or feel like crying. Like you feel when you get in trouble or skin your knee.

I want you to know
that it's okay to feel sad
sometimes, because that's what
happens when we miss someone
we love. You don't need to hide
your tears or act like you don't
miss me. Your tears are saying
"I love you" and letting me know
how special I am to you.

There may be times when you think of
me and feel mad at me for leaving you.
Like you feel when someone teases you
or takes away your favorite game.

I understand why you may feel
mad. Your world feels different
without me and you want things
to be back like they used to be.
I wish they could be too.
If I could have stayed with you
forever, I would have.

There may be times when you think of me and feel really lonely. Like you feel when you aren't invited to a friend's birthday party or have no one to play with.

I want you to know that it's okay to be alone sometimes. This special quiet time gives you the chance to daydream, relax and play make-believe. Maybe you'd like to become a superhero or live in a castle with a pet dragon. If you feel like writing me a letter or drawing a picture, I've left you some pages at the end of this letter to do just that.

There may be times when you think of me and don't understand why I am gone. Like you feel when you are told you can't play at a friend's house or can't figure out a new math problem you learn at school.

I want you to know it's okay to be confused.
As you get older and wiser, it will become
easier for you to understand—I promise.
You may not know how you are feeling right
now; you just know it doesn't feel good.

On the days you feel extra sad, please let an adult or trusted friend know. Talk with them and share stories about our times together. Everybody loves a good story and our stories are the best.

A great big hug from someone you care about can also help you feel warm inside and remind you that you are loved very much and not alone.

Oh how I loved getting those hugs from you.

If you want to do something in memory of me, you can plant a flower or a special tree in our backyard. Maybe you can donate my food, toys, or bed to an animal shelter—I have lots of special friends there. Or, have you ever watched bubbles twirl and swirl and float higher and higher until they look teeny tiny then disappear? Up, up, up they go!
If you want to blow bubbles in memory of me
I'll be watching for them . . .

Most importantly, don't forget that you can
talk to me anytime because remember I'm here
in your heart and I will hear you, even if it's just
a whisper. For the rest of your life, even when
you're old and gray, I'll still be with you.
I will comfort you in your sorrow and bark
and jump at your triumphs. I will eagerly
wait for each of your tomorrows.

I want you to know
that I am happy,
really happy,
where I am now.

This doesn't mean
I don't miss you like
crazy, or wish I could
come back to you,
but it's important to
me that you know
I AM OK.

It's so beautiful and peaceful here, where I am, far away among the stars. If we were here together, we would see flowers that we've never seen before and their scents would remind us of sliced lemons, grape Kool-Aid and freshly mowed grass.

We would stop and stare in wonder at our surroundings and enjoy the warmth of the brightest, bluest sky. Then we'd want to stop and splash in the sparkling rivers and lakes and lie down in the colorful meadows to watch the animals play.

I have made many new friends
with all different kinds of animals.
There is no "Big Bad Wolf"
as you've read about in
Little Red Riding Hood
or *The Three Little Pigs.*

We are all one big, loving family at this place
we now call home. We play together all day long
and take lots of naps. Remember how I loved
my naps? Now I nap on clouds as fluffy as
the cotton candy you get at the fair!

At night, as we lay on our warm, soft beds, we
talk about that one special friend we left behind.
I want you to know, when I share my story,
it is you I talk about.

I couldn't have felt more loved. You forgave me
when I was sometimes naughty, you were patient
with me as you tried to teach me new tricks,
and you always shared your popcorn with me.

But most of all, you were always so kind to me.
Please be as kind to yourself and to others as you
were to me. Being kind is really, really important.

As I drift off to sleep and look up at my favorite little star, I share my wish that you continue to always love with your whole heart, forgive easily, stay patient and share with others when you can.

You did all of those things for me, from
the very first day we met, and I want you
to know how much that meant to me and
what a difference it made in my life.

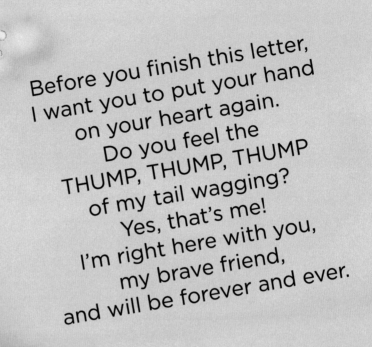

Before you finish this letter,
I want you to put your hand
on your heart again.
Do you feel the
THUMP, THUMP, THUMP
of my tail wagging?
Yes, that's me!
I'm right here with you,
my brave friend,
and will be forever and ever.

With Love,
Your Best Friend

Good Night Brave Friend

Please know when you lay down to sleep
I'll be resting here right at your feet
If you should wake throughout the night
I'll let you know that you're all right
And when the morning sun peeks in
A new day you will see
I'll be there with you all day long
Just like you were for me

Canis Major, nicknamed "the greater dog" in Latin, is a constellation seen in the Southern Hemisphere's summer or the Northern Hemisphere's winter sky. Canis Major was one of the most important constellations in ancient times because, as the brightest star in the night sky, Sirius, is part of it. Sirius is the nose of the dog and known as the "dog star." The expression "dog days" refers to the period of time from July 3rd through August 11th, when Sirius rises in conjunction with the sun. Canis Major is counted among the 88 modern constellations.

Dear Parents,

I encourage you to go back through the story and help your child find the constellation Canis Major illustrated throughout the book. As described above, it contains the brightest star in the night sky. How ironic it is that our precious pets are also our "brightest star" during our time with them on earth. If you would like to memorialize and have your very own star named after your beloved pet, please follow the link on my website at: www.mourningtolightpetloss.com/canismajor.

Dear _____,

I miss the times when . . .

_____

_____

_____

_____

_____

_____

Dear _____,

When I am sad I will . . .

_____

_____

_____

_____

_____

_____

Dear _____,
When I am alone I will . . .

_____

_____

_____

_____

_____

_____

Dear _____,
I know I will be okay because . . .

_____

_____

_____

_____

_____

_____

Dear _____,
Thank you for teaching me . . .

_____

_____

_____

_____

_____

_____

Dear _____,
My favorite memory of you is . . .

_____

_____

_____

_____

_____

_____

Place Favorite Pictures Here

This picture is special because . . .

_____

_____

_____

_____

_____

_____

This picture is special because . . .

_____

_____

_____

_____

_____

_____

This picture is special because . . .

_____

_____

_____

_____

_____

_____

Acknowledgments

I wish to express my love and appreciation to my husband, Andy, for your encouragement and belief in my work; to my children, Heather Plantt and Heidi Gerk for your loving, constant support and for your patience with my early morning phone calls to run ideas by you. To my amazing friends, you know who you are. What would I ever do without you? You have been my biggest cheerleaders and I love you all dearly.

I want to acknowledge and send out a HUGE thank you to the remarkably strong women of What If? Ideation and Publishing. Robin Shukle, managing editor, your professional insight, guidance and education will be used throughout my lifetime. Liz Mrofka, design and production, your talent and creativity amaze me! I could watch you for hours doing "what you do." A special thank you to my illustrator, Trish Murtha, for understanding my words and vision and turning them into meaningful, beautiful

illustrations. Words of gratitude also go to my editor, Catherine Cattarello. You did a wonderful job of editing my book and were a pleasure to work with.

Lastly, I want to thank my loving, sweet therapy dog Gracie. The tenderness and love you show to my clients and family are indescribable. How lucky are we that we get to work together? I couldn't ask for a better partner or friend. You have blessed my life immensely.

About the Author

Leigh Ann Gerk MA, LPC has been in the counseling field for over ten years. She is certified in Pet Loss & Grief Companioning and the founder and owner of Mourning to Light Pet Loss providing individual and family counseling for anyone grieving the loss of a pet. She currently offers 3 free pet loss support groups in Northern Colorado and is excited to branch out and offer more. Having grown up on a farm, Leigh Ann's childhood playmates included baby calves, horses, bunnies, dogs, and 32 cats that set up house in a boxcar that also served as her playhouse. This upbringing introduced her, at a very young age, to the human-animal bond and instilled in her a deep understanding of, and love for, this extraordinary relationship. Leigh Ann and her husband, Andy, live in Loveland, Colorado, and are the proud parents of identical twin daughters, Heather and Heidi. Their family is made complete by their cherished therapy dog, Gracie.

Visit Leigh Ann online at www.MourningToLightPetLoss.com.

About the Illustrator

Trish's illustrations are filled with the same whimsy and love that have drawn people to her award-winning watercolors for 30 years. Here in her first children's book, Trish's picture story is based on favorite people, places, memories and lessons learned growing up and with her three extraordinary adult children, five "grands", family and friends—furry and otherwise. She has worked in design, publication and writing and illustration since college plus her infectious, creative teaching fills classes, retreats and workshops for all ages. She migrates to New England from her Colorado studio—more stories from a road less traveled. Email: trishjourneys@gmail.com

Made in the USA
Middletown, DE
01 April 2023

28102723R00029